The Girl Who Lost Her Country

Written by
Amal de Chickera and Deirdre Brennan

Illustrated by
Dian Pu

A Publication By
THE INSTITUTE ON STATELESSNESS AND INCLUSION

The Institute on Statelessness and Inclusion is an independent organisation
committed to realising the right to a nationality for all.

© Institute on Statelessness and Inclusion, May 2018
info@institutesi.org
www.institutesi.org

Written by: Amal de Chickera and Deirdre Brennan
Illustrated by: Dian Pu
Designed by: Deshan Tennekoon
Published by: The Institute on Statelessness and Inclusion

Additional picture credits: pictures on pages 4, 25, 26 & 55 © SOS Villages Aboisso and UNHCR Cote d'Ivoire;
painting on page 77 © Kanchini Chandrasiri. Additional images (cropped to fit) under CC licence by Hazize San, Vanessa Porter, Cheryl Marland,
Jerome Bon, Rey Perezoso, Diyar Se.

Photo credits: photos on pages 17, 23, 52, 53, 55, 59 & 75 © Greg Constantine; photos on pages 31, 56 & 57 © Saiful Huq Omi; photo on page 21 ©
Allison Petrozziello and OBMICA; photo on page 42 © Subin Mulmi and FWLD; photo on page 83
© Deepti Gurung; photo on page 39 © The Kenya Human Rights Commission; photo on page 20 © Laura Quintana Soms; and photo on page 33
© Helen Brunt.

ISBN: 978-90-828366-0-8

The Institute on Statelessness and Inclusion is a non-profit foundation (Stichting)
incorporated in the Netherlands. Chamber of Commerce Registration Number: 61443840.

N is for Nationality,
S is for Statelessness
... and...
N is for Neha,
S is for Supergirl

*This book is for you and all the other children
around the world who have been made stateless
and then left to build your lives.*

We stand with you.

Table of Contents

Neha's Travels

I'm

falling,

falling,

falling!

Jerk!

Gasp!

Why do I always land with a jerk?
Every single time! I know it's a dream, but it still terrifies me.

I feel out of breath. I don't open my eyes.

I can feel a cold sweat all over my body. I then feel a steady pattering on my cheeks. Wet. Had I left the window open?

My hand scrunches up the sheet, but it crumbles into a million grains and slips through my fingers. Is that sand of some sort?

A hand jostles my shoulders. "Wake up" says a strange voice.

Raindrops fall on my face and bicycles whizz past. I am outside. Everything is strange and it's a little cold. I have never been here before.

I close my eyes. I must still be dreaming.

"Wake up!" The voice persists.

I cautiously open my eyes.

A boy, who is very fair and has blond hair, is staring at me. He must be about 12 years old, like me.

He looks as surprised as I feel. But he has good manners. He straightens up and says, "welcome to the **Netherlands**! I am **Lucas**."

I manage a feeble "hi I'm **Neha**, from **Nepal**", followed by "how did I get here?"

He looks perplexed and shrugs his shoulders.

We are in a small park, across the street from a row of houses. I stare mesmerised at the many cyclists travelling along. We both laugh when a man, looking at his phone, walks onto a special path for the bicycles and a chorus of bells startles him. He leaps back like a frog!

Lucas finally says, "come on, let's go inside". I'm glad to get out of the rain. We cross the road and he knocks on the door of one of the houses. A little girl opens it, his sister, **Linde**.

"So you are from Nepal, and you don't know how you got here to the Netherlands?"

I shake my head.

Silence.

I can see that Lucas is puzzling this all out in his head, eyebrows furrowed as he concentrates hard. I myself feel too dazed to do anything or think clearly.

He finally straightens up and says "I think I might know what brought you here! You may not believe me though". I guess my look says, "try me"! He puts his hand into his pocket and pulls out a coin. "Recognise this?" It's a Two **Rupee** coin from Nepal.

"I am a money collector... I mean, I collect coins" stutters Lucas. "I love to travel, and my coins are from some of the amazing places I have been to, or would love to go to.

THE NETHERLANDS IS A COUNTRY IN EUROPE AND ITS NAME CAN LITERALLY BE TRANSLATED AS "LOWER COUNTRY" BECAUSE OF ITS LOW AND FLAT LAND. IN FACT, SOME PARTS OF THE NETHERLANDS ARE ACTUALLY BELOW SEA LEVEL

THE RUPEE IS THE TYPE OF "CURRENCY" OR MONEY USED IN NEPAL AND SOME OTHER SOUTH ASIAN COUNTRIES LIKE INDIA AND SRI LANKA.

I've always wanted to go to Nepal, to climb the **Himalayas** and see the **Yeti**!"

"Now here's the crazy part. I wanted to go there so badly that I took this coin and held it in my palm and wished really, really hard to be able to see Nepal. Now you won't believe this, but when I opened my eyes, *puff*, you appeared!"

"I know it sounds crazy, right?"

I don't know what to say. His story *does* sound crazy. But how on earth had I ended up in the Netherlands, so far away from home?

Lucas then says something very wise. "My grandmother always told me that if something unexpected happens, it is for a good reason. I really wanted to travel and made a wish with my coin. But my coin brought you here instead. So, maybe, you need to travel more than I do!"

THE HIMALAYAS ARE THE TALLEST MOUNTAIN RANGE IN THE WORLD. THEY ARE IN INDIA, NEPAL, BHUTAN, CHINA AND PAKISTAN. THE HIGHEST MOUNTAIN ON EARTH, MOUNT EVEREST, IS IN BOTH NEPAL AND TIBET. THE YETI OR 'ABOMINABLE SNOWMAN' IS A CREATURE FROM FOLKLORE WHO SUPPOSEDLY LIVES IN THE HIMALAYAS. THEY SAY HE IS LIKE AN APE, BUT BIGGER.

Do I need to travel?

I am very happy at home in Nepal.

Or am I?

It all comes back to me now...

I had been at school with my Mom and elder sister Nikita. Mom was really upset, she kept telling the teacher that Nikita and I are Nepali, we were born there and had never even set foot outside the country. But the teachers were just shaking their heads. Miss Bhattarai wouldn't look my Mom in the eye. She stared at the ground saying "I am sorry **Didi,** but Nikita cannot sit her exams without showing proof of nationality."

'DIDI' IS A FRIENDLY WORD USED IN NEPAL BY WOMEN TO ADDRESS OTHER WOMEN. IT MEANS 'OLDER SISTER'.

Seeing my mother like this, I felt helpless. My mind immediately went to the other times I've seen her really unhappy like this. There was that time she was speaking to the rude man in the government office, trying to keep calm while she explained that my father was not there. Or the time when the judge in the court asked her a strange question about morals, which she did not answer.

My Mom loves us more than I thought was possible. She does everything for us. I could not bear seeing her like this. And worse, I could not bear to think that it had something to do with us.

Things went blurry and I felt dizzy. There was a sharp ringing sound in my ears. I could see people moving their lips but couldn't hear them.

My legs went wobbly and my eyelids closed.

The last thing I saw was Mom's feet.

I tell Lucas what happened. My last memory from Nepal. I tell him all the questions that I had spinning in my head at the time. "Why can't Nikita sit her exam? Will I also not be allowed? Is that why Mom was so upset? What is a nationality? Is everyone supposed to have one?"

He furrows his brow in the now familiar way. I feel like I've known him for much longer than a few minutes!

"I think a nationality is your origin, and where you are from. For example, if you are born in Germany then your origin is German. I think everyone has a nationality, because everyone has an origin. Everyone has a place they are from."

Linde, who had been silently listening to this all, then chips in: "hmm, nationality is the language you speak. I speak Dutch so I know I'm from the Netherlands. I have a bus card to get from my home to school and that has my name on it. So that probably proves I have Dutch nationality."

That makes me think.

I know I am from Nepal, I speak Nepali, so I must have Nepali nationality. But I also know Mom is having difficulty proving our nationality. And we don't have bus cards in Nepal!

"That's it! Your mission is to find your nationality!"

Lucas runs to his room and comes back with a little purse. "I keep my most precious coins here" he says. "Take it. I think the coin brought you here for a reason. I think that the coins will take you to places, so you can meet new people and learn about nationality. Take out a coin, squeeze it tightly, close your

11

eyes and make a wish. I think each coin will take you back to its own country. Find out more about nationality. Have a great adventure. And remember to tell us all about it!"

Linde then scrambles through her school bag and pulls out a notebook. "Here you go Neha! You can write your adventures and the answers to your questions in this book!"

QUESTION 1

WHAT IS A NATIONALITY? DOES EVERYBODY GET THE NATIONALITY OF THE COUNTRY WHERE THEY WERE BORN?

Okay so nationality seems to be where you are from and what language you speak. It seems like everyone has a nationality. But if this is true, why does my sister have problems?

I am so grateful. They are so nice. I thank them and hug them. I take the notebook and coins. I promise to let them know what happens. I close my eyes, pull out a random coin, clutch it close to my chest and make a wish.

～

There's a nice breeze, but boy is it hot! I can hear a bird singing… no I shouldn't call it singing, it's more like a shout or a shriek. "Caw-caw, caw-caw". I unclench my fist and I see 10 Rupees. But this is not Nepal. There are also two other languages engraved on the coin, that I can't read. I turn the coin round and see I am in **Sri Lanka**. Then I see it. The sea!

I have never seen the sea before. It's huge and it keeps on moving, but it doesn't go anywhere. I'm mesmerised.

SRI LANKA IS A BEAUTIFUL ISLAND IN SOUTH ASIA. IT IS SOMETIMES CALLED THE PEARL OF THE INDIAN OCEAN. SRI LANKA WAS ONCE RULED BY PORTUGAL AND THE NETHERLANDS AND THEN BRITAIN. IT FINALLY GAINED INDEPENDENCE IN 1948. OVER 20 MILLION PEOPLE FROM DIFFERENT ETHNIC GROUPS AND RELIGIONS LIVE IN THE COUNTRY.

Two girls jump in front of me and break my stare. They are sisters. Kenolee is nine years old and Kithmi is 10. We go and sit in the sand on the beach.

The buildings of **Colombo** – the capital city - are behind us.

I tell them my story. Kithmi thinks for a long time when I ask her "what is a nationality". She then says, "nationality is the different types of cultures and traditions and religions and different types of people in the world". Kenolee butts in, "not just that **Akki**. Like, erm, it means you have a… it's like a place. It's like a country you were born in, and the rules you follow. Like, my nationality is Sri Lankan so I need to follow the rules. Yeah. That's what it is."

AKKI MEANS 'OLDER SISTER' IN SINHALESE.

Kenolee goes on to say she knows she has Sri Lankan nationality "because I have been told that I have it. Plus you can feel what your nationality is. Like an energy. For example, you can feel you are Sri Lankan, or English, or American… like the energy that your body gives you. Oh, and plus, your skin colour."

I think about this. I tell Kithmi and Kenolee that I feel Nepali, I am part of the culture and I sometimes feel that "energy". I also look like other Nepali people so I don't understand why my mother cannot prove we are Nepali. Kithmi shrugs her shoulders.

WHAT ARE SOME OF THE RULES IN YOUR COUNTRY? (THESE ARE ALSO CALLED LAWS)

"Grownups can be weird" she says. I laugh in agreement, but I think she notices my sadness. She hugs me and says, "everyone has to have a nationality. Everyone has a homeland." We chat for a while and play catch on the beach. I then sadly tell them I should go. Kithmi tells me to wait a minute. She runs to her bag and returns with a small black object. "This is my travel camera - you can take 12 pictures with it. Use it wisely!"

DOES EVERYBODY GET A NATIONALITY IF THEY FOLLOW THE CULTURE, TRADITIONS AND RULES OF THE COUNTRY THEY LIVE IN?

I'm in a very ornate town square. There appear to be statues everywhere. Perhaps more than there are people! They all seem to be of big muscular men, riding horses or fighting with swords. I have never seen anything like it.

The coin I have in my hand says something in a language and script I do not understand. I have no clue where I am! The sun is beaming down and I am drawn to the huge water fountain in the middle of the square. There is a very tall pillar in the middle of the fountain and on it, a massive statue of a man riding a horse. Sitting on the wall of the fountain is a short woman. She looks to be the same age as my Mom and wears a colourful scarf around her face just like Mom does when we go for long walks in the forest near our house. "**T'aves baxtalo**" she says with a wide smile. I spot some missing teeth. "Welcome to Skopje, **Macedonia**". I remember studying about Macedonia in my history lessons. Isn't this where Alexander the Great was from? Perhaps that's why there are so many statues!

'T'AVES BAXTALO' MEANS 'WELCOME' IN THE ROMANI LANGUAGE. CAN YOU RESEARCH THE WORD FOR 'WELCOME' IN FIVE OTHER LANGUAGES?

Kezia introduces herself to me, she tells me she is a Romani woman and has seven young children, three sons and four daughters. She has lived in Macedonia all her life but has only been living in Skopje, the capital city, for the last ten years. Roma people are one of Europe's oldest and largest **ethnic minorities** she tells me. They face many difficulties in life. People can be very mean to them and judge them. This reminds me of people in Nepal who are treated very badly. Like the **Dalits**.

Kezia is very kind. Perhaps this is because she knows how it feels when people are unkind to her. She says that she too is struggling to prove she and her

family are from the country they were born in.

"Except for my youngest daughter, none of my children have been registered. I have six undocumented children. I gave birth to my youngest daughter in hospital, that's why she was registered. I gave birth to the others at home, that's why they are not registered."

"If one of my children gets ill or hurt, I always have to beg the doctors at the hospital to treat them for free, because I have no money to pay. I think that if my children had birth certificates they would treat us much better."

Kezia says that **birth registration** is important to show that her children were born in Macedonia. If her children grow

DALIT PEOPLE ARE CONSIDERED TO BE A LOWER 'CASTE'. THE CASTE SYSTEM IS A WAY PEOPLE MARK DIFFERENCES BETWEEN VARIOUS GROUPS. IN THE OLD DAYS, YOUR CASTE WAS BASED ON THE JOB YOU DID. BUT NOW, IT IS OFTEN JUST USED TO TREAT SOME PEOPLE AS MORE IMPORTANT, AND OTHERS AS LESS IMPORTANT. THE WORD 'DALIT' MEANS 'OPPRESSED' IN THE ANCIENT SANSKRIT LANGUAGE. MANY DALIT PEOPLE ARE STILL TREATED BADLY, EVEN THOUGH IT IS AGAINST THE LAW TO DO SO.

up without birth registration they may never receive Macedonian nationality. She tells me that there are millions of children all over the world who cannot receive a nationality. "When no country will accept a child as their national, then that child is **stateless**."

I feel a little dizzy as the word "stateless" circles around in my mind. Are Nikita and I stateless?

State-less?

Without a state?

Without a country?

Is this possible?

Kezia explains why she has never had Macedonian nationality herself. "My mother did not have money for hospital fees when I was born. And so, the hospital did not give her the papers confirming my birth. My birth was never registered. Maybe she could have fought for my nationality in the government offices - I wish she had demanded it. But she could not read or write and going to those places, full of people with serious faces and expensive clothing was scary for my mother. I understand that now. I too never had the chance to go to school and I don't have the confidence to demand my rights from people more educated and more powerful than me."

She tells me that many parents pass down secret family recipes to their children, or give them money or a house to live in, but all she has passed on to her children is an uncertain future. "My children will inherit statelessness from me. I cannot get a job because I do not have an identity card. I collect plastic bottles and cardboard to make some money. I want my children to receive a nationality and live a better life than me."

I can feel a lump in my throat as Kezia talks. There are also tears in her eyes. She takes photos out of her handbag to show me her beautiful children. I take a picture of one of her photographs. It's two of her sons staring into the camera. They look pretty cool, and also a little cheeky. I think that if I met them, I would like them.

After some time passes, the sun starts to set. We hug each other and say goodbye. She wishes me well. I say I will keep her family in my heart.

I feel my stomach drop as it hits me, I think I am a stateless person. I wonder if my birth was registered, and I also wonder if birth registration alone is enough to prove where I belong.

I go through my now familiar coin ritual, shaking the purse before I pick one out. I wonder where I will be taken next.

~

A beautiful, kind, warm face is looking down at me. I learn that it belongs to Rosa, and I am in the **Dominican Republic**. In my hand is a one **Peso** coin. We are sitting on white plastic chairs under

QUESTION 3

IS IT YOUR BIRTH CERTIFICATE THAT GIVES YOU A NATIONALITY?

the shade of a tree. Next to me are three little girls. Rosa tells me they are ten, eight and three. They are playing "elastics" together (a game in which you jump in figures on and off two elastics stretched around a tree).

I tell her my story, and how I fear I may be stateless. Rosa reaches towards me and squeezes my two knees affectionately. "Neha, you are so welcome my dear. I would like to share our story with you. Maybe in the future you will tell it to someone else. I will be happy when more people know about us, who have been made stateless."

Rosa tells me that she used to have the nationality of the Dominican Republic but that it was taken away from her a few years ago. "Yes sweetie, some people are born stateless and will try all their lives

to get a nationality. But others, like us, once had a nationality which was taken away. You see, the government made a new rule in 2013 that children or grandchildren of **immigrants** from Haiti, who could not show certain documents, would not be Dominican citizens, even though they had been born in the Dominican Republic. The older, better rule, was that anyone born in the Dominican Republic had Dominican nationality. So this change was very confusing and unfair."

"My own father moved to the Dominican Republic from **Haiti** when he was nineteen. He worked in the fields, cutting sugarcane. He worked really hard and made a new life for himself here. He met my mother at a dance and married her. He was a beautiful caring man who worked hard to make sure we had school books and could get the education he never got. His heart would break if he were alive today and knew his granddaughters and I are no longer accepted here, the place he considered home. He would feel sick to know that without nationality his granddaughters can no longer go to school. I haven't even been allowed to register the birth of my youngest daughter! When I gave birth to her in the hospital they wouldn't give me her birth certificate. Yesterday, someone told my eldest daughter to 'go home' when she was on the bus. My eyes filled with tears when she asked me 'Mom, why don't they want us? What did we do?' We haven't done anything wrong but there is a lot of racism and **discrimination** here. In the Dominican Republic, people whose ancestors were from Haiti are treated badly. They say we have darker skin and we are poor and dirty and we don't belong. It is very hurtful. My whole life I have been Dominican. This is what I am. I have never even been to Haiti."

"What will you do?" I ask Rosa. She pauses, her brown eyes sparkling. She glances at her children who are still playing together and giggling, and then she smiles proudly. "We will fight for our nationality dear. We have been making films and plays to raise awareness about this bad law and what it is like living without a nationality. Having a nationality is our right, and we will continue to protest in the street until our voices are heard and we have our nationality back."

She is such a brave, wise and kind woman. I take a picture of her children, who by now have been joined by some other kids as well. They are all very special. I then join the kids and play with them. Rosa gives us fresh coconut water

to drink, it barely touches my lips as I gulp it down in the tropical heat.

Just before I leave, Rosa's daughter Talia hands me a beautiful drawing on pink paper (you can see it on the next page).

Rosa explains: "on the left, Talia shows how she feels. 'When I do not have a birth certificate and my sister or mother go to run errands to try to get papers and they do not appear, I feel sad. If I don't have my birth certificate I will not be able to study.' On the right, she has drawn herself as 'Queen of Misfortune' alongside the text 'when I have it I will feel happy because I will be able to finish my schooling.'"

I am angry that little children all over the world like Talia face such situations. It's not just Nikita and myself. I feel I must learn more and do something to make their lives better!

People can lose their nationality! That just sounds crazy! Rosa's daughters went to school every day until one day that was all taken away from them. That gets me thinking…

I am in a large garden. There are lots of trees, and the ground is patchy, some grass and lots of soil. It clearly is a garden that sees lots of activity! I check the money in my hand. It says 10 Francs. But I'm not in France. In fact, France does not use Francs anymore, it uses Euros. But the money of **Cote d'Ivoire**, which was a former French **colony**, is still called Francs.

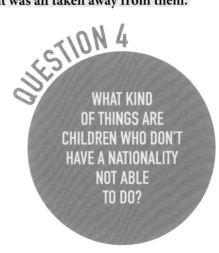

QUESTION 4

WHAT KIND OF THINGS ARE CHILDREN WHO DON'T HAVE A NATIONALITY NOT ABLE TO DO?

WHY DO PEOPLE WHO HAVE A NATIONALITY SOMETIMES LOSE IT?

I befriend a little girl called Grace. She is dark skinned, has a cute button nose and her hair is in braids.

"Hi Neha, welcome to the SOS Children's village, welcome to my home."

She shows me around the grounds of the orphanage. Tall palm trees are dotted around the land, and little houses sit on top of bright green grass. Two children run past us playing chase and I notice a group of kids and a woman sitting at a table on the veranda of a house.

I think they're doing school work.

"I don't know who my parents are, where I am from or where I was born. I think my parents lost me when I was born, and someone brought me here. I think I am about 12 years old, but I can't be sure."

I think Grace is beautiful, and I take her picture:

Grace explains to me that in Cote d'Ivoire it is very hard to get nationality without your parents' documents. "Ivorians must provide their birth certificate, and the nationality certificate of a parent, as proof of their own nationality. I don't have any of those things Neha and I cannot prove that my parents were Ivorian. They call me a **foundling** and I have heard some grownups say that I am stateless".

"If, one day, I can no longer go to school, I would be very unhappy", she says. "In Cote d'Ivoire stateless people cannot do many things, like working or opening a bank account, they can't own land or even move freely inside the country. My dream is to travel"

COTE D'IVOIRE WAS ONCE A COLONY OF FRANCE. A COLONY IS A COUNTRY THAT WAS INVADED AND RULED BY ANOTHER COUNTRY. WHILE UNDER FRENCH RULE, SOME FRENCH PEOPLE SETTLED IN COTE D'IVOIRE. FRANCE HAD ALSO COLONISED NEIGHBOURING BURKINA FASO, AND PEOPLE FROM THERE WERE FORCED TO COME TO COTE D'IVOIRE TO WORK ON PLANTATIONS. AFTER COTE D'IVOIRE BECAME AN INDEPENDENT COUNTRY IN 1960, MANY OF THESE PEOPLE ORIGINALLY FROM BURKINA FASO, AND THEIR DESCENDANTS, CONTINUED TO LIVE THERE.

23

she says, "I would like to explore the capital Abidjan, and discover other countries. I want to become Minister of Finance. I would like to be a powerful woman and help others. That would make me happy."

This gets me thinking. Shouldn't it be easy for countries to accept children as their nationals, even if they don't have birth certificates? How silly, to say you don't belong, just because you don't have a piece of paper? Where do these countries expect these children to go? What do they expect them to do?

QUESTION 6

WHY CAN'T COUNTRIES MAKE SURE ALL CHILDREN GET A NATIONALITY, EVEN IF THEY DON'T KNOW WHERE THEY WERE BORN OR WHO THEIR PARENTS WERE?

Grace and I sit with the children I spotted earlier, they're still working at the table. Malik, one of the boys hands me the piece of paper he is drawing on. His face is soft but he has a deep, pumpkin seed-shaped scar under his eye which makes me wonder what his life has been like. On his piece of paper is a drawing of people queuing up to register for a nationality card. I really like his picture and take a photograph of it.

I also take pictures of a couple of other really nice paintings that the other kids have drawn.

Malik tells me that he also doesn't know who his parents are. He doesn't remember them. He can't get any kind of identity documents without a father or mother.

I take a piece of paper and some crayons and join in…

Grace and I end the day lying side-by-side swinging in an old hammock. We are eating slices of melon and examining each other's art. I apologise for leaving a smudge stain from my sticky fingers on her drawing. Grace's picture has loads and loads of little dots on it. She runs her hand over the page and explains to me what it means to her.

"Maybe one child without nationality is okay, maybe she finds a family to adopt her and can get nationality from them. But look Neha, this is all of us,

25

there are thousands and thousands of us, the lost children of Cote d'Ivoire. This place is my home, our home. I… we have never known anywhere else, and I want them to accept us as their children. I will give back so much to this country if I have the chance, if I could just go to school and get a job. We would all do so much, I know we would."

We fall asleep under the stars.

I wake up in a dimly lit path. It is very smelly. There are flies buzzing around and garbage everywhere. It is dawn. It is cool but I sense it will soon get warm. Once I get accustomed to the light and my surroundings, I notice a thin little child peeping at me. He is bare bodied and wearing an old pair of shorts. He is shy, but curious.

"Hello" I say. He smiles and runs away, so I follow. He is kicking an old plastic bottle as he runs, and when I catch up, he kicks it to me. I kick it back and we both laugh.

"My name is Neha, I'm from Nepal."

He looks down.

"What's your name? Where are you from?"

No response.

I try again. "Where are we?"

"Kutapulong" he says, and when he sees my quizzical look he adds, "Bangladesh".

I look at the coin in my hand, it is a Bangladeshi **Taka**.

"Oh OK. So you are Bangladeshi?"

He looks down and shakes his head.

"Where are you from?" I ask again.

"Myanmar."

"Oh, so you're Burmese?"

Again he shakes his head. "They call us Bengali, and say we are from Bangladesh. But we are **Rohingya**. We are from Myanmar. That is our home."

"So why did you leave?" I ask… half dreading what his answer may be.

"They chased us out" he says. "They burnt our homes and shot at us. It was terrible."

I am shocked and don't know what to say.

Luckily, he keeps on talking. "Our village was beautiful. But now it is all burnt. I don't know if I will ever be able to go back. I'm afraid I will forget it, so every time I close my eyes, I try to remember exactly how it looked and smelt. How can they say that someone who knows exactly how a place looks and feels, is not from there? I don't understand."

I am trying to make sense of this. Does he have a nationality or is he stateless? And why had he been chased away from his country? Would that happen to me too?

I ask him if he was the only one who ran away. He beckons to me and takes me to a clearing. It is then that I realise we are on a small hill. He points below. There is a sea of shacks, huts and tents – as far as my eyes could see – all crammed full of people. There must have been gazillions!

ROHINGYA PEOPLE ARE AN ETHNIC MINORITY WHO HAVE LIVED FOR CENTURIES IN MYANMAR. MYANMAR IS A VERY DIVERSE COUNTRY, WITH PEOPLE FROM MANY ETHNIC AND RELIGIOUS GROUPS. HOWEVER, MANY PEOPLE IN MYANMAR DO NOT ACCEPT THE ROHINGYA. THEY ARE NOT RECOGNISED AS NATIONALS OF MYANMAR – THEY ARE STATELESS. THE ROHINGYA ARE TREATED VERY BADLY, PERHAPS WORSE THAN ANY OTHER STATELESS GROUP IN THE WORLD. AND SO, HUNDREDS OF THOUSANDS OF ROHINGYA HAVE FLED MYANMAR, TO BANGLADESH, MALAYSIA, THAILAND, INDIA, PAKISTAN, SAUDI ARABIA AND OTHER COUNTRIES.

"This is our home now" he says, "because they say we are not from there".

I feel tears coming into my eyes, but I do not want to make him sad, so I decide to change the subject. "Do you like football?" I ask. "Come let's play. I will be the goalie".

Later on, I take his photograph. He has a very beautiful smile.

I take out my notebook and write in it.

After he has left, I realise that I never learnt his name. He is nameless, just like his people, whose name "Rohingya" is not recognised in their own country.

QUESTION 7

WHAT HAPPENS TO STATELESS PEOPLE WHO ARE TREATED SO BADLY THAT THEY HAVE TO RUN AWAY FROM THEIR COUNTRY?

I feel very bad. I hope I will see him again, so I can ask.

I close my eyes, open my purse and pull out a coin…

⁓

The ground is wobbling underneath me. I feel a little queasy. It takes a little time for me to figure out what's happening. I finally realise that I'm on a long wooden boat that's rocking from side to side. Beside it is another boat, and there's a wooden house, and another, and another. Some of the boats and houses are linked together by planks of wood, ladders and nets, and there are children running quickly from one to the other. It reminds me of the **slum** neighbourhood in Kathmandu, there are even skinny dogs mooching around. My coin says **Ringgit** and tells me I am in **Malaysia**. I know that not too long ago, Malaysia had the tallest building in the world. But I never knew it had villages built on the sea!

A crowd of children come skipping towards me. I smile nervously and blurt out "I can't swim". "It's okay" says one of the children who is dressed in a ripped and dirty t-shirt and shorts, "we're professionals". The other kids laugh. A taller boy says, "we are the Guardians of the Sea and we will protect you". The shorter boy, Aasif, hands me something that looks like a sausage and tells me to try it, "it's sea cucumber". I swallow a bit but my stomach already feels like wobbly jelly and I can't finish it.

Aasif and the other children tell me that they are **Bajau Laut**. "We live on these boats... and we work here".

SLUM IS USUALLY THE WORD USED TO DESCRIBE A RUN-DOWN AND OVERCROWDED AREA IN A CITY WHERE POOR PEOPLE LIVE. IT MAY NOT HAVE GOOD FACILITIES SUCH AS TOILETS OR RUNNING WATER AND SO IT CAN BE VERY DIRTY.

MALAYSIA IS A COUNTRY IN SOUTHEAST ASIA. IT IS MADE UP OF TWO SIMILARLY SIZED REGIONS, 'PENINSULAR MALAYSIA' AND 'EAST MALAYSIA' THAT ARE SEPARATED BY THE SOUTH CHINA SEA. MALAYSIA WAS ONCE COLONISED BY THE BRITISH. IT HAS MANY ETHNIC GROUPS, RELIGIONS AND CULTURES. THE FOOD IN MALAYSIA IS GREAT!

"You *work* here?" I ask. "Yes we have to help our parents, we don't go to school so sometimes we go fishing or pound cassava or rice."

I later learn that they cannot go to school because Malaysia does not recognise them as nationals.

Riki, has a wide smile and her hair is tied up in a cotton wrap. She's wearing a dress that is too big. She tells me how she and her siblings have never set foot in another country, but Malaysia still won't accept them.

"The government thinks Bajau Laut are Filipinos" she says. "So even before I was born, my fate was decided. I would be stateless. I would inherit statelessness from my parents, who inherited it from my grandparents."

BAJAU LAUT (ALSO KNOWN AS THE SAMA DILAUT) ARE A COMMUNITY OF PEOPLE WHO MOSTLY LIVE IN BOATS ALONG THE COASTLINE OF SABAH IN MALAYSIA. THEY DEPEND ON THE SEA FOR THEIR FOOD AND FOR WORK.

Aasif hands me a fishing rod and shows me how to cast it. He tells me that he hasn't seen his dad in two years, "because my dad doesn't have any kind of identity card the police arrested him and took him away. I heard my Mom say that he is probably in a prison somewhere but I know from my friends that they tried to send some to the Philippines. I hope they haven't sent my dad there. He has never lived there. He won't know anyone." I am still feeling queasy, so we move onto land. Riki shows me how she helps her mum grind rice by pounding it on a carved-out stone with a big pole. I give it a go. The pole is extremely heavy! It's amazing how she does this. She is such a strong girl. I take her picture!

This has been an amazing

adventure. I never knew that people lived on houses in the sea. And these kids are such a friendly and fun bunch. You would never know that they face such hardship, that they cannot go to school, they work hard and some of their parents are even in prison. All of this is because they are stateless.

It's now time for me to go. I say goodbye to my new friends and go through my coin ritual again.

The sweet and citrusy smells of cardamom and boiling rice fill my nostrils as I open my eyes. I'm sitting in a kitchen, a slim woman with shiny brown hair plaited into a French braid vigorously stirs a pot. Four pots sit bubbling, steaming and sizzling on top of the gas cooker. The woman expertly keeps her eyes and hands moving across all four of them. "Can you pass me the onions Sima" she says to the girl playing a board game on the other side of the room.

Sima, ignores her mother, picks up her board game and runs over to me.

"Hello! Who are you?" By now I have telling my story down to a fine art… they all gather around me and listen. I am in Germany, as my **One Euro** coin tells me. I remember Lucas talking about being born in Germany. Wouldn't he love to know I am almost back to where I began?

"Neha" Sima says giggling. "In Arabic Neha means love and rain! Isn't that so weird? Who loves the rain?" I burst out laughing. I tell her that even in Nepali it means love and rain, but also eyes. In fact, my Mom would always tell us that to her, "Neha" means "beautiful dreamy eyes" and "Nikita" means "warrior princess"!

Sima asks if I'll play "Guess Who" with her before dinner is ready. As I try to guess which card Sima has and ask her yes/no questions like "does your person wear glasses?" she tells me that she doesn't really speak Arabic, but she tries. She speaks Kurdish mainly, especially with her family at home. And she tries her best to speak German and English. She loves languages and tells me to ask her my "Guess Who" questions in Nepali.

Sima, her parents and I sit on the floor in the sitting room. In front of us is a spread of all the delicious things Sima's mum Lorana had been cooking. My tummy is rumbling. There are little balls of fried dough. I'm not quite sure what is inside them, the flatbread looks so fluffy and the rice, dotted with the fragrant cardamom seeds, has a crispy layer on top – I've never seen rice served like this before but I'm dying to take a bite.

Sima and her family are Kurdish Syrians living in Germany. Over dinner her dad Sami explains to me: "we are **Kurds**, I was born in Syria, like my wife and my children, and we lived there all our lives before the war broke out. However, not one of us has Syrian nationality. Neha, we are "**maktoum**", this means we are not registered in Syria. When a **census** was carried out in 1962 many Kurdish Syrians were not registered. My grandfather was on bad terms with his landlord at the time and when the census committee visited his landlord he did

THE EURO IS A CURRENCY USED IN 19 COUNTRIES IN EUROPE. EACH COUNTRY HAS ITS OWN DESIGN ON THE REVERSE SIDE.

MANY (BUT NOT ALL) NAMES HAVE SPECIAL MEANINGS. HAVE YOU EVER LOOKED UP THE MEANING OF YOUR NAME? WHAT DOES YOUR NAME MEAN IN THE LANGUAGE YOU SPEAK AND WHAT DOES IT MEAN IN OTHER LANGUAGES?

not pass on my grandfather's name for registration. My grandfather instantly became stateless and we have had to inherit this status and pass it down to our own children ever since."

Lorana passes me more **dolma** and says "We have told our story to many different people. Researchers come to collect our stories and tell us they will write them in a book, we were also filmed once for a documentary but we haven't seen the film. If you tell others about us, Neha, please tell them our message is to other parents. I ask mothers to imagine how it feels to know that the child they gave birth to is not registered in their name."

I feel sad and angry. My mind drifts back to my own mother. I suddenly worry that she may be missing me. How long have I been away? But I must find all the answers I came for!

Sima's dad holds his wife's hand and says "you try to do everything for your children, and yet somehow you know you are not able to give them everything that other children have. This feels horrible."

They then tell me a little about life in Germany, that they have been able to send Sima to school but they still feel like they are searching for a place to call home. "We have been here for two years and we really hope that we will receive German residency."

"We are **refugees** because of the war, but we are also stateless. If we ever go back to Syria will they recognise us as their own?

Syria has never accepted us before. We pray that Germany will."

~

I am in a big field. There are lots of people singing, dancing, drumming, laughing. It's hot and sweaty and full of life and happiness. I unclench my fist, the coin in my palm is a Kenyan **Shilling**. I have always wanted to travel to **Kenya**, I cannot believe my luck!

There's an amazing energy in the field. A man sees me and calls me into the dancing crowd. "Welcome, my young friend" he says. "Come join our celebration."

I ask him what they are celebrating. He laughs and says "we are finally recognised by our country. We are the Makonde. We were stateless, but we marched to **Nairobi** to meet the president and demand our rights. We are now citizens!" I am amazed, and I burst out laughing in pure joy. I immediately find myself thinking, 'so this is a fight we can win'.

I spend some time in the field, talking to and celebrating with the Makonde people. I learn that they were first brought from Mozambique to Kenya by the British in 1936. Despite living there for generations since, they were later treated as foreigners. On various occasions they were promised that they would be registered, but this never happened, and they faced many hardships. Felistus, a gentle and soft-spoken woman told me how when she was a child, her mother once had to carry her up a cashew

A REFUGEE IS A PERSON WHO SEEKS PROTECTION IN ANOTHER COUNTRY. A REFUGEE IS FORCED TO LEAVE THEIR OWN COUNTRY FOR VARIOUS REASONS, FOR EXAMPLE, BECAUSE THEIR LIVES, SAFETY OR FREEDOM ARE THREATENED BY VIOLENCE AND DANGER.

QUESTION 8

IF THE GOVERNMENT REFUSES TO GIVE YOU NATIONALITY, OR TAKES YOUR NATIONALITY AWAY, WHAT CAN YOU DO TO CHANGE YOUR SITUATION?

KENYA IS A WONDERFUL COUNTRY IN EAST AFRICA. IT IS VERY DIVERSE, WITH DIFFERENT ETHNIC GROUPS. KENYA TOO WAS A COLONY OF THE BRITISH, WHO BROUGHT PEOPLE FROM NEIGHBOURING COUNTRIES TO KENYA. MANY OF THESE COMMUNITIES FACED STATELESSNESS. NAIROBI IS THE CAPITAL CITY OF KENYA.

nut tree at night to hide away from the police. Dahili, a very fit looking football player told me how he missed a sponsorship opportunity to play football in Europe because he didn't have identity documents.

One of the elders, Thomas says, "finally we realised we were in a tight place in life. We looked for people to educate us on how to get our rights".

Peter jumps in, "we made a decision that we need to march to Nairobi to meet the president. We had tried all legal processes. Yet no one assisted us. We gathered in Makongeni in the coast region, started with prayers and then began our march."

In total, the Makonde trekked 526 kilometres, until they reached the president's house in Nairobi. They faced many challenges on the way. They were even stopped by the police. But they kept on going. Amina shows me a photograph of the march. It looks amazing, and I wish I had been there to support them!

Peter continues: "once we got to Nairobi, there were challenges. We were blocked again by many police officers who were heavily armed. Due to our unity and solidarity, we had no fear. We knew we had not done anything wrong in fighting for our rights."

I am in awe of these wonderful, brave people. But the most amazing thing is that the president finally did meet them, and he asked for their forgiveness, because it took such a long time to bring justice to them as fellow Kenyans.

By now, there is a small crowd around me, and they all chip in with how they feel.

Sylvester, an old man says "they made us forget all the pain. We are grateful and happy that we are Kenyan citizens."

Amina adds, "even though I don't have anything, at least I have an identity card. You just feel like breathing. Haaaaaah. You breathe well now."

What an amazing experience. I feel fully energised and confident to fight for my rights in Nepal too. I will never forget Peter's parting words to me: "I have got my rights and I will succeed because I am a winner!"

Before I open my eyes I know where I am. The sound of busy roads and cars beeping, the thick, dusty air and the heavy heat of the sun on my black hair is so familiar to me. I'm home!

I can't wait to see Mom, to hug her and tell her everything I've learned. But as I open my eyes I see I'm not back at my village. I'm standing outside an office building in **Kathmandu**, the capital city.

I go in.

"Namaste **bahini**", a tall, smartly dressed woman bows slightly and I bow in return, hands pressed together, palms touching and fingers pointing upwards – this is our Namaste greeting in Nepal. Sushma Gautam tells me to hurry inside. Once in the reception room, Lila, a stumpy woman wearing an apron, with a nose piercing and silver bangles up both of her arms, asks if we would like some **chiya**. I can't wait to drink it again after being away for so long. I tried so much fantastic food from all over the world, but the spices and creaminess of chiya brings me comfort like nothing else.

Sushma aunty brings me into her office; I look at the leaflets on the desk -- I'm in an organisation that works for women's rights and helps people fight for citizenship.

Sushma aunty takes out her laptop and shows me a picture of young Nepali girls and boys protesting on the streets of Kathmandu. "Neha, you know that women and men, girls and boys, are equal, right?" I nod my head vigorously. "Well, in most countries around the world men and women are considered to be equal and their equal rights are protected by the **constitution**" she says. "However, it is sad that in reality, the opposite can be true. Women make up half the world's population, but in most countries, they do not make up half the people employed in the government, or in technology and media jobs. They also often make less money than men, even for doing the

BAHINI MEANS YOUNGER SISTER IN NEPALI, BUT IT IS ALSO A FRIENDLY WORD USED BY WOMEN TO ADDRESS OTHER YOUNG WOMEN AND GIRLS.

CHIYA, ALSO KNOWN AS CHAI, IS A SPICED TEA COMMONLY DRUNK IN SOUTH ASIA. IT IS MADE BY BREWING BLACK TEA, MILK AND SUGAR WITH SPICES, LIKE CINNAMON, CLOVES AND GINGER.

A CONSTITUTION IS THE SET OF MAIN LAWS OF A COUNTRY. IN MOST COUNTRIES, THESE ARE WRITTEN DOWN IN ONE PLACE, AND THEY SET OUT HOW WE MUST TREAT EACH OTHER AND OTHER IMPORTANT RULES.

same job. At home, women are more likely than men to carry out chores and look after children – even if both men and women work full time jobs."

Sushma aunty continues, "in **25 countries**, women still don't have equal rights with men to give their nationality to their children. Nepal is one of these countries. Neha, your mother raised you and Nikita by herself but, despite this, she still has to prove who your father is and that he is also Nepali so that you can both receive Nepali nationality. Many government officials have very bad attitudes towards women. They don't treat women with the same respect as men. When your mother went to register Nikita at the district office she was told that she had to bring Nikita's father with her because *'children should get their nationality from their father.'* This isn't true though, and they were very wrong to treat your mother like that."

I realise I am slowly shaking with anger. I remember the rude man in the government

HAVE YOU EVER FELT THAT WOMEN ARE TREATED DIFFERENTLY TO MEN? DO THEY DO MORE WORK AROUND THE HOUSE OR ARE THEY EXPECTED TO DO DIFFERENT KINDS OF JOBS? WHAT DO YOU FEEL ABOUT THIS?

office, the judge in the court and the teacher in school. I think of everything my mother has had to go through, just because my country thinks it's OK to treat women badly. I think of my friends around the world who are also suffering because of bad laws and bad attitudes.

I ask Sushma aunty if this means I will grow up without a nationality.

She says "we, as lawyers, have helped many people in your situation. We will help your mum fight this case in the Supreme Court so that you and Nikita can grow up with Nepali nationality, in your mother's name, as is your right."

I feel a swell of emotion and gratitude towards this woman I have just met. I decide that I too will become a lawyer, so I can continue to help people get the nationality they deserve.

Sushma aunty tells me that the people in the picture are part of a group called "Citizenship in the Name of the Mother" and that they too are being denied the right to receive nationality from their mothers. Most of them haven't been able to get a job since they left high school, some of those who did were treated badly and never received their wages. She said without nationality you can't even buy a sim card for your phone. The group want to put pressure on the government to change the law. They protest outside government buildings every Friday. On my way home in the taxi, I write my final thoughts on this fascinating, colourful, exhausting, inspiring, educational, tasty adventure:

I feel Nepali.

I was born in Nepal, I celebrate all the traditions of Nepal, I speak perfect Nepali. But because of the law and some people's attitudes, my sister Nikita and I are not accepted as Nepali. But there is no other country that would recognise me as their national, or which I would want to be a national of (though I would love to visit them all). I have never lived anywhere else, my mother is Nepali, my grandparents were Nepali. If Nepal does not recognise me as Nepali, I am stateless.

Nationality is a funny thing, not everyone understands what it is. Most people have one, but some people don't.

I used to think everyone had a nationality, that you have the nationality of the country you are born in. But I realised I was different when my Mom found out Nikita couldn't finish her school exams. I now know that being officially recognised by a country as a national, and having a piece of paper, like a birth certificate, identity card or passport is so important for so many things. Without it Kezia can't bring her children to the hospital if they are sick. Rosa's children cannot go to school and may not have opportunities for good jobs. Grace may never be able to fulfil her dreams of travelling. Sima and her parents continue to search for a country that accepts them. And my sister and I must wait to find out if we can finish our schooling.

We can change this, and we must. People like Sushma aunty are working hard every day, to fight for everyone's right to nationality. There have been some great successes. For others, it is taking longer. And so, more of us need to join the fight. We must do everything we can, so that every child does have a nationality!

I am home now, looking into my mother's eyes. They are dark hazelnut and could trick me into thinking I am looking into the eyes of my sister. Her strong arms, and her hands, wide, flat, a little hardened on the palm, squeeze me closely to her. Those are the hands that cooked every meal for us when we grew up. She would always make food from different countries, sushi from Japan, Indian samosas, American potato salad. She gave us everything we wanted but now there is one thing she can't give us.

I tell her about all the children and parents I met around the world.

She is silent, tears in her eyes.

She finally says "stateless. My children are stateless. Because I decided to raise you on my own, without your father's support. Because I decided to educate you and inspire you to be good human beings. I am a Nepali citizen and I am a single mother. But because I am a woman I do not have the right to pass on my name or my nationality to my children."

~

It's been a few weeks now since my adventure. I flick through my notebook and all my pictures. I have made some amazing friends and I have written to all of them. They all agree with me that it's very silly that there are children and adults who don't have a nationality. It is also very harmful. This should be such an easy problem to solve, if only grownups would all agree that no one should be stateless.

My friends from around the world and I are going to fight for everyone's right to a nationality. We will learn more about what needs to be done and all fight for our right, and for our families' right to have a nationality and to live free from discrimination. We will continue to share our stories so that others can learn the importance of nationality and why we must fight to end statelessness. We hope you will join us too!

The World of

Pacific ocean

North America

Atlantic Ocean

South America

I CAN'T BELIEVE
I TRAVELLED TO SO
MANY COUNTRIES. I GOT
THIS WORLD MAP AND COLOURED ALL THE
COUNTRIES I WENT TO IN RED. CAN YOU
NAME THEM ALL? MY MAGICAL COINS REALLY
DID TAKE ME ALL AROUND THE WORLD!

SINCE MY GREAT ADVENTURE, I HAVE
ALSO LEARNT SO MUCH MORE ABOUT
STATELESSNESS. I HAVE COLOURED
IN YELLOW, SOME OF THE COUNTRIES
IN WHICH I HAVE LEARNT STATELESSNESS
IS A PROBLEM. CAN YOU NAME ALL OF
THE YELLOW COUNTRIES ON THE MAP?
CAN YOU RESEARCH OR THINK OF OTHERS?

Statelessness

Neha's Questions

HERE ARE THE QUESTIONS I WROTE DOWN IN MY NOTEBOOK. HOW WOULD YOU ANSWER THEM?

QUESTION 1

WHAT IS A NATIONALITY? DOES EVERYBODY GET THE NATIONALITY OF THE COUNTRY WHERE THEY WERE BORN?

QUESTION 2

DOES EVERYBODY GET A NATIONALITY IF THEY FOLLOW THE CULTURE, TRADITIONS AND RULES OF THE COUNTRY THEY LIVE IN?

QUESTION 3

IS IT YOUR BIRTH CERTIFICATE THAT GIVES YOU A NATIONALITY?

QUESTION 4

WHAT KIND OF THINGS ARE CHILDREN WHO DON'T HAVE A NATIONALITY NOT ABLE TO DO?

QUESTION 5

WHY DO PEOPLE WHO HAVE A NATIONALITY SOMETIMES LOSE IT?

QUESTION 6

WHY CAN'T COUNTRIES MAKE SURE ALL CHILDREN GET A NATIONALITY, EVEN IF THEY DON'T KNOW WHERE THEY WERE BORN OR WHO THEIR PARENTS WERE?

QUESTION 7

WHAT HAPPENS TO STATELESS PEOPLE WHO ARE TREATED SO BADLY THAT THEY HAVE TO RUN AWAY FROM THEIR COUNTRY?

QUESTION 8

IF THE GOVERNMENT REFUSES TO GIVE YOU NATIONALITY, OR TAKES YOUR NATIONALITY AWAY, WHAT CAN YOU DO TO CHANGE YOUR SITUATION?

THROUGH MY TRAVELS AND MY RESEARCH, I MET SOME REAL EXPERTS ON STATELESSNESS. I WAS ALSO ABLE TO ASK SOME OF THE PEOPLE WHO STUDY AND WORK ON THIS ISSUE IF THEY WOULD ANSWER MY QUESTIONS. HERE IS WHAT THEY SAID!

QUESTION 1

WHAT IS A NATIONALITY? DOES EVERYBODY GET THE NATIONALITY OF THE COUNTRY WHERE THEY WERE BORN?

Having a nationality is like holding official membership of a country. It offers a sense of belonging – to a place and to a community. This is why people often support their national team in sports competitions like the Olympics or World Cup. Because they all feel like they belong, and they want their country to do well.

Each country has its own rules about how you can become a member: rules (or laws) that set out which people are granted nationality. Some countries give nationality to anybody born there. Other countries give nationality to anybody who has a parent from the country. Most countries allow people who have lived there for a long time or married someone from the country, to apply for nationality. In this way, the real-life connections that a person has with a country form the basis for becoming a national.

There is a very important document called the **Universal Declaration of Human Rights**, which sets out the rights of every single person in the world. The Declaration says that **"everyone has the right to a nationality"**. This means that nationality rules should be fair and everyone should be able to get a nationality somewhere. No one should be stateless.

However, some countries have bad rules, like not allowing women to pass on their nationality to their children or saying that people who belong to certain minorities cannot have nationality. Other countries have good rules that are not practised properly. For all of these reasons, there are still many people in the world who do not have a nationality.

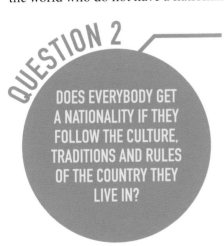

QUESTION 2

DOES EVERYBODY GET A NATIONALITY IF THEY FOLLOW THE CULTURE, TRADITIONS AND RULES OF THE COUNTRY THEY LIVE IN?

Everyone should have a nationality. This does not (or should not) have much to do with whether they follow the culture, traditions or rules of the country they live in.

However, not everyone does.

No one knows the exact number, but we think that at least 15 million people around the world are stateless. Normally, if a person does not have a nationality, it is not because they have done something wrong. Nor is it because they have failed to follow the culture, traditions or rules of a country or do not have a real connection to it.

It is usually because the country has done something wrong – because it has bad rules, or gaps in them, or has not properly practised its rules. Sometimes, these are mistakes. But sometimes, they are deliberate, because the country discriminates against certain types of people.

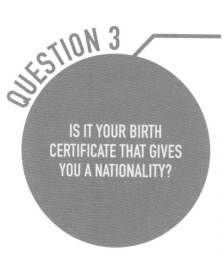

QUESTION 3

IS IT YOUR BIRTH CERTIFICATE THAT GIVES YOU A NATIONALITY?

A birth certificate is not the same as a nationality. There are many children in the world whose birth has not been registered but who still have a nationality because they have a connection to a country. However, a birth certificate is a very important document: it proves where you were born, when you were born and who your parents were. Usually, these are the links that help figure out what your nationality is (or should be). And so, it becomes more difficult for people who do not have birth certificates, to prove their nationality.

Now have a look at this picture:

This is a young boy in Serbia. He is holding, what is to him, the most precious piece of paper in the world. Before his father died, he gave him this paper. On it, he had written the names and birth dates of the boy and his six brothers and sisters. None of these seven children had their births registered. There is no official record of their births, so they cannot prove that they should have Serbian nationality. If their births were registered they would be able to prove their link to the country.

QUESTION 4

WHAT KIND OF THINGS ARE CHILDREN WHO DON'T HAVE A NATIONALITY NOT ABLE TO DO?

The same way the Universal Declaration of Human Rights protects everyone's right to a nationality, it also protects our other rights as well. Another very special document – the **Convention on the Rights of the Child** – also sets out how children must be treated and protected, and what their rights are. According to these documents, children have a right to a nationality. But importantly, children who don't have a nationality should still have all their other rights protected. For example, they

53

should be safe, be able to go to school, see a doctor when they are sick, play, be with their families and carers, and they should not have to work.

But as we have heard, many children without a nationality are not able to do these things. This is clearly wrong, it goes against every child's rights, and must be changed.

Many children who do not have a nationality are not able to go to school. Or even if they are, they are not allowed to finish their exams. When they are sick, they sometimes cannot see a doctor or go to hospital. Sometimes they have to work, like the child in the picture on page 53, and this can be very hard and even dangerous.

Life can be very difficult for children who don't have a nationality. It is never their fault that they do not have a nationality, and it is incredibly unfair and sad that they are treated badly.

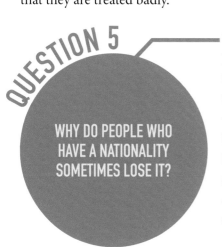

QUESTION 5

WHY DO PEOPLE WHO HAVE A NATIONALITY SOMETIMES LOSE IT?

We saw that Rosa and her family in the Dominican Republic, lost their nationality because a bad new law was made. They belong to an ethnic minority group, and their country decided to treat that minority badly. Children who are affected by these bad laws, like those in this photograph, can see their whole future change before their eyes because they are no longer recognised as members of their country.

There are other countries that have also taken away the nationality of entire groups. Myanmar for example, took away the nationality of Rohingya people and Syria of many members of the Kurdish community.

Another reason you can lose your nationality is if the country you live in, splits up into two or more countries. The Soviet Union used to be the biggest country in the world. But in the early 1990s, the Soviet Union split up into 15 new countries. People who had been nationals of the Soviet Union, suddenly, were required to get the nationality of the new country they were in. Most of them did, but some, even today, have no nationality because each new country set its own rules and some people were not included.

Some countries have decided that they can take away nationality of people who do very bad things. People who join wars against their own country, or become terrorists, can lose their nationality. These are, of course, difficult problems for a country to deal with, but if someone has done bad things, they should be punished under the law, the same way people who commit murder are punished. There is no need for them to have their nationality taken away. There is also no proof that this makes countries any safer. There are other problems too. Sometimes, these laws are used in a wrong way, for instance by a government that decides to take away the nationality of people who are activists and who have not done anything wrong. Also, in some countries, the children of parents who lose their nationality like this, can also lose their nationality.

WHY CAN'T COUNTRIES MAKE SURE ALL CHILDREN GET A NATIONALITY, EVEN IF THEY DON'T KNOW WHERE THEY WERE BORN OR WHO THEIR PARENTS WERE?

All countries *can* and *should* make sure children get a nationality, even if they don't know where the children were born or who their parents were. They can do this by making a very simple change to the nationality law of the country. For example, a law can say "Any foundling discovered in Sweden shall be considered to be a Swedish citizen". This is called a "safeguard against childhood statelessness" – it is a special rule that is only needed in cases where a child is not able to get a nationality through the regular rules that exist. Unfortunately, there aren't enough countries that have such a system in place. Even those that do, do not always put these safeguards that exist on paper into practice. The baby in this photograph was born in Malaysia, to stateless Rohingya parents. If Malaysia acted on a safeguard in its law – to provide nationality to children born in the country who would otherwise be stateless - this baby would receive Malaysian nationality. But because Malaysia does not, this child will also be stateless.

WHAT HAPPENS TO STATELESS PEOPLE WHO ARE TREATED SO BADLY THAT THEY HAVE TO RUN AWAY FROM THEIR COUNTRY?

When people are treated really badly and their lives are in danger because of how they look, or their religion, or what they believe in, this is called **persecution**. Sometimes, people are persecuted for the same reasons that they are not given a nationality. Many people who are persecuted are forced to run away, leaving their homes and belongings and everything they love behind. Having to run away like this is a very difficult and sad thing to have to do.

When people run away to a whole new country, to find safety, they become **refugees** – like the girl in the photograph below, who is crossing the border from Myanmar to Bangladesh.

It requires bravery to leave all that is familiar behind and go to a new country where you don't know the people and sometimes don't even speak the language. The word "refugee" comes from the word "refuge" which is a place of shelter. It basically means, "A person who has run away to another country, to escape persecution".

The world has agreed that it is wrong to persecute people, and it is right and important to protect refugees. But more work is needed, to teach people to respect each other, talk to each other and to not harm others. Similarly, we need to make sure that those who are harmed and need protection from harm, receive that protection. We can all help to make refugees feel welcome and safe.

QUESTION 8

IF THE GOVERNMENT REFUSES TO GIVE YOU NATIONALITY, OR TAKES YOUR NATIONALITY AWAY, WHAT CAN YOU DO TO CHANGE YOUR SITUATION?

If your country doesn't recognise your nationality, or takes it away from you, there are some things that you can do to try and change your situation. In most countries, with the help of a lawyer, you will be able to ask the courts to decide if you have been treated fairly or not. This may help you to find a solution to your problem. But, if the law itself is a bad one, the courts may not be able to help. Then, it will be more difficult. But there are lots of people who are fighting around the world, for everyone's right to a nationality. They are running campaigns, speaking to leaders, protesting and doing all kinds of interesting and important things to change the situation. As we saw with the Makonde, these campaigns can be successful. But they can also take a very long time and hard work! The photograph on the opposite page is of some men protesting in Kuwait. They are Bidoon. They deserve Kuwaiti nationality and have been fighting for it for many years.

Questions by

AS I LEARNT ABOUT MORE SITUATIONS OF STATELESSNESS FROM AROUND THE WORLD AND STARTED MAKING FRIENDS WITH MORE YOUNG PEOPLE WHO THEMSELVES ARE STATELESS, I STARTED RECEIVING QUESTIONS FROM THEM. MANY OF THEIR QUESTIONS WERE VERY DIFFICULT FOR ME TO ANSWER. THEY REALLY MADE ME THINK. SOME OF THEM ALSO MADE ME VERY ANGRY, THAT EVEN TODAY, CHILDREN HAVE TO ASK SUCH QUESTIONS ABOUT THEIR OWN LIVES. HOW WOULD YOU ANSWER THESE QUESTIONS?

Why don't I have nationality, although I was born in this country?
– *Bakhrom, 14 years old, Kyrgyzstan*

Why is it that a person like me, who is the second generation born in Madagascar and who has no link with any other country, cannot have Malagasy nationality? – *Mohamed, 14 years old, Madagascar*

Do I look any different than anyone here? How do I ask a question, when everything I plan about my future ends with endless questions?
– *Subhashini, 12 years old, Malaysia*

Stateless Children

Why is it that my brothers have documents,
but (like so many other girls) I do not?
– *Zalina, 19 years old, Tajikistan*

How long will I have to wait to have
equal rights with other people? I have been
fighting for this my whole life.
– *Phra, Thailand*

What will happen if I never continue
my education beyond this year?
– *Sheellin, 15 years old, Malaysia*

Does the world care about us?
How much longer must I wait?
– *Andrew, South Africa*

EVERY PERSON HAS HUMAN RIGHTS. WE HAVE THESE RIGHTS BECAUSE WE ARE HUMAN, AND WE BELIEVE THAT EVERYONE HAS DIGNITY, IS EQUAL AND SHOULD BE FREE. THIS MEANS THAT NO ONE SHOULD TAKE OUR RIGHTS AWAY FROM US. EVERYONE SHOULD RESPECT OUR RIGHTS, JUST LIKE WE SHOULD RESPECT THE RIGHTS OF OTHERS.

Know Your Rights!

ONE THING I HAVE NOW LEARNT, IS THAT EVERY PERSON IN THE WORLD HAS **RIGHTS**, FROM THE YOUNGEST NEW BORN BABY TO THE OLDEST GREAT-GREAT-GRANDMOTHER.

AFTER THE SECOND WORLD WAR, THE COUNTRIES OF THE WORLD CAME TOGETHER TO SET UP THE **UNITED NATIONS** (UN). THROUGH THE UN, THEY TRY TO ENSURE THAT WE LIVE IN PEACE AND DIGNITY, AND THAT NO ONE FACES THE MISERY OF WAR AGAIN.

ON THE 10TH OF DECEMBER 1948, THE UN AGREED ON A VERY IMPORTANT DOCUMENT CALLED THE **UNIVERSAL DECLARATION OF HUMAN RIGHTS**. THIS DOCUMENT SETS OUT THE RIGHTS THAT ALL PEOPLE HAVE, REGARDLESS OF WHO THEY ARE OR WHERE THEY LIVE. SINCE THEN, OTHER AGREEMENTS HAVE ALSO BEEN MADE TO PROMOTE AND PROTECT EVERYONE'S HUMAN RIGHTS. BUT EVEN TODAY, THE UNIVERSAL DECLARATION IS RECOGNISED AS THE CORNERSTONE OF HUMAN RIGHTS. EVERY 10TH OF DECEMBER IS CELEBRATED AROUND THE WORLD AS **INTERNATIONAL HUMAN RIGHTS DAY**.

I'M SURE YOU WILL AGREE THAT CHILDREN ARE THE MOST IMPORTANT PEOPLE IN THE WORLD. THEY NEED EXTRA PROTECTION AND CARE. THAT IS WHY, IN 1989, THE **CONVENTION ON THE RIGHTS OF THE CHILD** WAS AGREED. THIS RECOGNISES THAT "EVERY CHILD IS BORN FREE AND EQUAL" AND SETS OUT THE SPECIAL RIGHTS THAT ALL CHILDREN HAVE. ALL BUT ONE COUNTRY IN THE WORLD HAVE SIGNED UP TO THIS DOCUMENT. THEY ALL PROMISE TO PROTECT THE RIGHTS THAT IT CONTAINS.

Here are the key rights that you hold, as a child, and that every other child also holds:

All children are equal and have these rights. You should not be treated badly or unfairly because of how you look, what you believe, where you live, what language you speak, whether you are rich or poor, whether you have a disability, whether you are a girl or boy; or who your parents or guardians are.

All adults and countries must do what is best for you and all other children.

Me   My Name   My Family   My Nationality   My Personality

You have the right to your own identity; a name, a nationality and to know your parents and family. No one should take this away from you. No child should be stateless.

You have the right to live with your family or carers.

You have the right to speak and say what you believe. Adults and other children should listen when children speak.

You have the right to discover things, learn and explore.

You have the right to be safe, to be protected from harm.

You have the right to the best healthcare possible.

You have the right to have food to eat, clothes to wear and a safe place to live.

You have the right to go to school, and to be able to learn.

You have the right to play, and the right to rest.

You should not have to do work that is harmful, dangerous, bad for your health or which prevents you from going to school.

You should never be treated badly or punished in a cruel or harmful way.

Help?

If you were to become a refugee, you have a right to special protection.

AS YOU CAN SEE, THE RIGHT TO A NATIONALITY IS ONE OF THE RIGHTS THAT EVERY CHILD HAS. CHILDREN WHO DO NOT HAVE A NATIONALITY, ARE OFTEN TREATED BADLY WHEN IT COMES TO OTHER RIGHTS AS WELL. THIS MEANS, THEY ARE BEING PUNISHED TWICE - FIRST BY DENYING THEM THE RIGHT TO A NATIONALITY, AND THEN BY DENYING THEM OTHER RIGHTS. IF THINGS GO WRONG, AND YOUR RIGHTS ARE NOT RESPECTED, THERE ARE THINGS THAT YOU CAN DO TO CLAIM YOUR RIGHTS. YOU CAN SPEAK ABOUT YOUR PROBLEM TO PEOPLE YOU TRUST, LIKE YOUR PARENTS OR TEACHERS OR FRIENDS. WITH THEIR HELP, IF IT IS A VERY SERIOUS PROBLEM, YOU MAY BE ABLE TO GO TO A HUMAN RIGHTS ORGANISATION OR LAWYER. MANY HUMAN RIGHTS ORGANISATIONS WORK TO PROTECT THE RIGHTS OF CHILDREN. THEY HELP CHILDREN OUT, RAISE AWARENESS ABOUT PROBLEMS, CAMPAIGN FOR CHANGE AND EVEN CHALLENGE BAD PRACTICES, DECISIONS AND RULES. YOU MAY EVEN MAKE A COMPLAINT TO A COURT, TO ASK A JUDGE TO MAKE AN ORDER THAT YOU ARE TREATED PROPERLY.
THERE IS ALSO A SPECIAL UN COMMITTEE OF EXPERTS WHOSE ROLE IS TO KEEP AN EYE ON WHAT COUNTRIES ARE DOING TO PROTECT THE RIGHTS OF CHILDREN: THE **COMMITTEE ON THE RIGHTS OF THE CHILD**. THIS COMMITTEE TALKS WITH GOVERNMENTS TO SEE WHAT CAN BE DONE TO IMPROVE HOW CHILDREN ARE TREATED. THE COMMITTEE ALSO LISTENS TO COMPLAINTS FROM CHILDREN IF THE SITUATION IS VERY BAD, TO SEE IF IT CAN OFFER A SOLUTION. ANYONE - ESPECIALLY CHILDREN - WHO FEEL THEIR COUNTRY IS TREATING CHILDREN POORLY, CAN SPEAK DIRECTLY TO THE COMMITTEE AND TELL THEM WHAT THEY THINK.

IF WE ALL KNOW OUR RIGHTS, WE CAN ALL PROTECT EACH OTHER'S RIGHTS BETTER!

Neha's Reflections

THROUGH MY TRAVELS AND ADVENTURES, ALL THAT I'VE READ AND THE EXPERTS I HAVE SPOKEN TO, I HAVE BEGUN TO LEARN A FAIR BIT ABOUT STATELESSNESS. THERE IS SO MUCH THOUGH, AND IT CAN BE COMPLICATED. SO I DECIDED TO DRAW IT ALL UP IN A WAY THAT MADE SENSE TO ME. HERE IT IS. I HOPE THIS MAKE SENSE TO YOU TOO!

Everyone has the right to a nationality. It doesn't matter who you are!

But countries can decide the rules by which people get nationality. These rules are usually based on who has strong connections to the country because...

- They were born there
- Their parents are nationals
- They live and work there
- They are married to or are adopted by nationals

But some countries have bad laws, or do not apply their laws correctly. And so...

- People who **should** have nationality are **denied** it
- People who **would** have nationality cannot **prove** it
- People who **do** have nationality can **lose** it

71

PEOPLE WHO HAVE NO NATIONALITY ARE **STATELESS**. THEIR RIGHT TO A NATIONALITY HAS BEEN DENIED. **ALL PEOPLE HAVE HUMAN RIGHTS**. THOSE WHO HAVE LOST THEIR RIGHT TO A NATIONALITY SHOULD NOT LOSE THEIR OTHER RIGHTS.

BUT COUNTRIES TREAT STATELESS PEOPLE BADLY. THEY DISCRIMINATE AGAINST THEM AND DENY THEIR RIGHTS:

- ROSA'S CHILDREN COULD NOT GO TO SCHOOL
- KEZIA'S CHILDREN COULD NOT GO TO HOSPITAL
- RIKI AND AASIF HAD TO WORK LIKE GROWN UPS
- AASIF'S FATHER WAS PUT IN JAIL AND MAY EVEN HAVE BEEN SENT TO ANOTHER COUNTRY
- DAHILI COULDN'T PLAY FOOTBALL ABROAD
- THE ROHINGYA WERE PERSECUTED

THIS IS WHY IT IS SO IMPORTANT:

- TO FIGHT FOR EVERYONE'S RIGHT TO A NATIONALITY
- TO PROTECT THE HUMAN RIGHTS OF EVERY STATELESS PERSON

SOME THINGS THAT WE CAN DO:

- MAKE SURE THAT EVERY CHILD RECEIVES A BIRTH CERTIFICATE
- MAKE SURE THAT EVERY COUNTRY HAS A SAFEGUARD AGAINST STATELESSNESS
- FIGHT AGAINST LAWS THAT DISCRIMINATE – ESPECIALLY AGAINST ETHNIC MINORITIES, WOMEN AND DISABLED PEOPLE
- PROTEST IF ANY COUNTRY TRIES TO TAKE AWAY SOMEONE'S NATIONALITY
- WELCOME AND PROTECT ALL REFUGEES

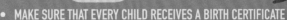

We See You

GREG CONSTANTINE IS A FAMOUS PHOTOGRAPHER, WHO HAS SPOKEN TO, AND TAKEN THE PICTURES OF HUNDREDS OF STATELESS CHILDREN AROUND THE WORLD. I WAS VERY LUCKY TO GET TO KNOW HIM THROUGH MY WORK ON STATELESSNESS. HE RECENTLY SHARED THIS REFLECTION WITH ME, WHICH MADE ME THINK OF MY FRIENDS GRACE AND MALIK. IT MADE ME EVEN MORE DETERMINED TO MAKE THINGS RIGHT. HERE IS WHAT GREG SHARED:

I remember travelling to Cote d'Ivoire. It was early 2010. I travelled all around the amazing country, meeting with stateless people who struggled every day. Most were born in Cote d'Ivoire but they were not recognised as citizens. And with that, they were denied documents and this paralysed them from being able to move forward with their lives, jobs, education and sense of belonging to this country they called home. Toward the end of my time in Cote d'Ivoire, I visited an orphanage in the capital of Abidjan. The orphanage was home to many children who had been given away at birth or orphaned because their parents had passed away. Some of them had been abandoned because they had a disability.

At the time, the laws in Cote d'Ivoire did not provide citizenship to children who were 'foundlings', a child who could not provide evidence of his or her parents. As a result, the child would travel through life stateless. One of these children was eleven years old. He had been stateless and had lived in the orphanage all his life.

I remember talking briefly with him and when I took his photograph, he said something to me in French. I don't speak or understand French. Before the translator told me what the young boy said, I expected he said something about me taking his photograph. But instead, the translator told me the young boy said…

"*You see me.*"

It was an incredibly powerful moment. One that I will never forget. Why? Because in so many ways, children are the most silent and invisible victims of statelessness. And without a doubt, children have the most to lose by statelessness as well. They represent futures denied. Potential denied. A wealth of amazing contributions to society denied. Children must rely on others for their voice, and this includes other children. Other children who know what it is like to go to school, enjoy their studies and discover the excitement that comes from learning and having an education. Other children who also have dreams but live day to day with the opportunity to make those dreams come true. Other children, regardless of where they are in the world, who believe it is important to say, "all children deserve a birth certificate. All children deserve the right to citizenship. All children deserve a future."

We see you!

Letter to a Stateless Child

AFTER MY MAGICAL JOURNEY, I GOT TO KNOW THREE WONDER-FUL WOMEN WHO HAVE COM-MITTED THEIR WHOLE LIVES TO HELPING PEOPLE, UNDERSTAND-ING HISTORY AND USING THE LAW FOR GOOD. THEY WERE VERY TAKEN BY MY STORY, AND THEY ENCOURAGED ME TO CONTINUE MY FIGHT FOR JUSTICE. THEY SAID I WAS VERY BRAVE AND WAS DOING AN AMAZING JOB. THEY ALSO SAID THAT THEY WOULD CONTINUE TO DO WHAT THEY CAN AS WELL. THEN THEY HAD A THOUGHT, THAT IT MUST FEEL VERY LONELY AND DESPERATE TO BE STATELESS, PARTICU-LARLY IF YOU DON'T KNOW THAT THERE ARE OTHER PEOPLE OUT THERE WHO ARE FIGHTING FOR CHANGE. AND SO, THEY DECIDED TO WRITE THIS LETTER TO A STATELESS CHILD.

Dear friend,

We are writing to you because you are one of very many children in the world who are stateless. Because you have no nationality, the world has treated you unfairly. This is not your fault, or your parents. Everyone is equal and should be treated equally. We firmly believe this and have spent many years working to achieve equality for all people.

The situation you are in, may be like <u>eight-year-old Elsa's</u>, who was born in the Dominican Republic. Her mother was born in Haiti but has lived in the Dominican Republic for many years; her grandmother is a citizen of the Dominican Republic. But Elsa is not recognised as a Dominican. She will only be able to go to <u>school</u> until she is 10. After that she will need identity papers.

Or <u>Ivan's</u>, born in Kosovo, the son of a Croatian mother and a Serbian father whose identity papers were destroyed during war. When Ivan was very sick, the hospital refused to admit him because he did not have identity papers.

Or <u>Subina's</u>, who was born in Nepal. Her mother was not married. In Nepal, it is difficult for an unmarried woman to pass her nationality to her child. Subina told us: "I had always felt the same as my friends until the day when I had to fill up my form for the School Leaving Certificate's board exam... all my friend's forms were accepted. Mine was not."

Or like many other children who have been made stateless for many other reasons. But remember, you are unique and special. Your story is your own. You are the future of the world and you will be able do great things, particularly if you are allowed to reach your potential. You probably ask if the world cares about you. How much longer must you wait? What can you do to make the world understand the situation you are in? We believe you have been let down. It is very unfair that you are treated in this way. Everyone has the human right to have a nationality – to fully belong to a country. This means that every boy and girl should have identity papers, including a birth certificate. All children have this right, no matter who they are, where they live, what their parents do (or whether they have parents), what language they speak, what their religion is, whether they are a boy or a girl, what their culture is, whether they have a disability, and whether they are rich or poor. This is a human right for every child, promised in the Universal Declaration of Human Rights, and in the Convention on the Rights of the Child.

But making this happen – achieving equality – is a battle which has had to be fought over and over again, by many people in every country, including our own.

One of our grandmothers lost her citizenship when she married a man from another country. Another of our grandparents was stateless because the government of their country did not count Jews as citizens. The parents of another of us, took in refugee boys in Europe who had to leave their own countries because they were being punished by a dictator. And all three of us have dear friends who have lost their citizenship or are themselves stateless.

There is no excuse for you to suffer because of who your parents are or what your religion is or whether your mother could pass her citizenship to you. You have human rights, and you should be able to enjoy them.

We want you to know that there are people trying to stop statelessness happening, and to change the situation of those like you who are stateless now. It is frustrating, most of all for you, that there are not yet enough of us. But we do see signs of progress, with more people coming on board and greater understanding of why children are stateless, and what it means to have no nationality. The United Nations is asking countries to change their laws, and some countries are beginning to do this. Ten refugee and stateless athletes led the opening parade at the 2016 Olympic Games in Rio de Janeiro, flying the Olympic flag, marching to the Olympic anthem, receiving a standing ovation by the entire stadium in honour of their talents and bravery.

Meanwhile we are awed by so many of you who are facing your situation with courage. We promise to continue working for you, and to encourage others to do so as well.

Rachel Brett, Stefanie Grant, Linda K Kerber

IF YOU HAVE A NATIONALITY, WOULD YOU THINK OF WRITING A LETTER TO A STATELESS CHILD? WHAT WOULD YOU SAY?

IF YOU ARE STATELESS, WOULD YOU THINK OF WRITING A LETTER TO A CHILD WHO HAS NATIONALITY OR TO A STATELESS CHILD IN ANOTHER COUNTRY? WHAT WOULD YOU SAY?

Neha's Future

My classmate suggested we have a picnic on Friday to celebrate the end of our exams. I ask Mom what she thinks I should make. *"Shamburak"* Mom says, "I saw a delicious recipe on YouTube recently and I really want to try making them, I can help you **Nanu**." Mom describes shamburak to me as fried dough stuffed with slow cooked meat, herbs and spices. Suddenly a wave of feelings rushes down my back and into my legs. I need to sit down. I can practically smell the spicy and citrusy aromas of Sima's house. "Mom, are they a Syrian Kurdish snack?" "Yes Nanu" she replies.

The last few years have been a whirlwind. My friends from around the world, Grace and Sima, Riki and Lucas and everyone else all did so much to raise awareness about nationality and statelessness. And we made so many new friends along the way. We would write to each other sometimes too, and they got to know each other through me. But something about the image and smell of this food has mentally transported me back into that adventure which started it all.

NANU MEANS YOUNG GIRL IN NEPALI

Recently, we finally received Nepalese nationality! It was a long battle. My mom would stay up late reading about similar cases going on in the Supreme Court in Kathmandu. We would protest outside government buildings every Friday after school. I even read a poem I wrote, about what it feels like to be stateless, in front of a large crowd of people in **Durbar Square**.

DURBAR SQUARE IS A VERY HISTORICAL AND BEAUTIFUL SQUARE IN KATHMANDU.

People from different countries would visit our house and ask us about our life. We must have been to the Supreme Court four or five times. Sometimes our case would be postponed and delayed.

Through this all, I felt trapped inside an invisible box; I could move, act, talk like a normal person but something out of my control and out of my sight was blocking me from becoming my full self.

Sushma aunty, our lawyer, was amazing. She argued that the citizenship law in Nepal went against the Constitution, which states that all men and women should be equal. We finally won our right to nationality. I'll never forget the day we received that news; I was so full of joy I wished the happiness I was feeling was contagious and could spread to everyone I knew.

The exams I'm taking are the same exams I feared so terribly my sister wouldn't be able to sit. I am only able to take these exams because I have a nationality. Even though exams suck, so much worry has cleared from my mind.

I now have a nationality. No one can take this away from me. I think of my friends around the world. I really, really want to see them again. To thank them for everything. To tell them that I will continue to fight for them and everyone else who still doesn't have a nationality.

I tell my Mom I'll be right back.

I run to my bedroom and from under my bed and behind some bags I grab a shoebox. Inside the shoebox and underneath the letters, photos and my tattered old notebook is Lucas' bag of coins.

I reach in. Without looking, I pick one out. I squeeze it tightly and wish my special wish.

I open my eyes but I'm still in my bedroom.

I drop that coin and try another one and then another one.

Nothing. Nothing.

And then it strikes me.

I don't need the coins anymore.

I am where I belong.

I am recognised.

I am equal.

Learn, Think, Act, Campaign, Play. Be Creative and Raise Awareness!

SO NOW YOU KNOW A LOT ABOUT STATELESSNESS. YOU PROBABLY KNOW MORE ABOUT STATELESSNESS THAN MOST PEOPLE IN THE WORLD! THAT MAKES YOU AN EXPERT! I HOPE YOU WILL HELP US TO TELL MORE PEOPLE ABOUT NATIONALITY AND STATE-LESSNESS, AND HOW UNFAIR AND WRONG IT IS, THAT SOME CHILDREN ARE STATE-LESS. THERE ARE LOTS OF THINGS YOU CAN DO!

For more information on things you can do to raise awareness about statelessness and be an activist for change, as well as for other great resources to learn about statelessness, check out this website: www.kids.worldsstateless.org

These are just some examples of things you can do.
Try different things. Find out what works for you. How can you best understand and communicate the feelings inside of you? Use your talents to raise awareness about statelessness and nationality. Teach other people what you have learnt. Make them also interested. Together we can make a difference!

LEARN MORE ABOUT STATELESSNESS IN YOUR COUNTRY. FIND OUT IF THERE ARE PEOPLE WHO ARE STATELESS. LEARN ABOUT THEIR HISTORY; WHAT HAPPENED AND WHAT THEY ARE DOING ABOUT IT.

BE A CAMPAIGN CHAMPION BY QUIZZING AND INFORMING AS MANY PEOPLE AS YOU KNOW ABOUT STATELESSNESS! START WITH YOUR FAMILY AND FRIENDS. SPEAK TO YOUR TEACHER AND CLASSMATES.

WRITE A LETTER TO THE EDITOR OF YOUR LOCAL NEWSPAPER, YOUR SCHOOL MAGAZINE OR TO A POLITICIAN. TELL THEM WHAT STATELESSNESS IS AND HOW THEY CAN HELP TO ADDRESS IT.

MAKE A SHORT VIDEO ABOUT STATELESSNESS AND WHAT CAN BE DONE ABOUT IT. SEND IT TO FRIENDS AND FAMILY BY SOCIAL MEDIA. REMEMBER THOUGH, ALWAYS STAY SAFE ONLINE!

MAKE A POSTER FOR YOUR HOME OR CLASSROOM ABOUT THE NATIONALITY LAW IN YOUR COUNTRY, EVERY CHILD'S RIGHT TO A NATIONALITY, OR THE RIGHTS OF ALL STATELESS CHILDREN.

COME UP WITH GOOD SLOGANS FOR CAMPAIGNING AND PROTESTS. "EVERYONE SHOULD HAVE A NATIONALITY" OR "NATIONALITY FOR ALL". CAN YOU THINK OF MORE?

PAINT A PICTURE ABOUT STATELESSNESS. USE A PHOTOGRAPH FOR INSPIRATION OR USE YOUR IMAGINATION. MAYBE YOU CAN ENTER IT INTO AN ART COMPETITION, OR FOR YOUR SCHOOL EXHIBITION!

IF YOU ARE FEELING VERY CREATIVE, WRITE A POEM OR A SHORT STORY OR A PLAY OR A SONG. YOU COULD PERFORM IT AT YOUR SCHOOL, OR IN FRONT OF FRIENDS OR FAMILY.

Acknowledgements

This book has been produced by the Institute on Statelessness and Inclusion (the Institute), an independent organisation committed to realising the right to a nationality for all. One of our main focuses has been the issue of childhood statelessness, which impacts millions of children around the world. This book, and its sister website www.kids.worldsstateless.org, aim to contribute to raising the awareness of children and adults alike, on this phenomenon that places so much unnecessary strain on so many young shoulders.

This book was written by Amal de Chickera and Deirdre Brennan, with additional editorial input from Laura van Waas and Ileen Verbeek. It was illustrated by Dian Pu and designed by Deshan Tennekoon. We are very grateful to the children of SOS Villages Aboisso and UNHCR Cote d'Ivoire for permission to use their paintings (pages 4, 25, 26 & 55) and to Kanchini Chandrasiri for her painting (page 77). We are also grateful to the photographers who generously shared their images with us: Greg Constantine (pages 17, 23, 52, 53, 55, 59 & 75), Saiful Huq Omi (pages 31, 56 & 57), Allison Petrozziello and OBMICA (page 21), Subin Mulmi and FWLD (page 42), Deepti Gurung (page 83), the Kenya Human Rights Commission (page 39), Laura Quintana Soms (page 20) and Helen Brunt (page 33). Our special thanks to Anne and Geoff Hayward, Piyumi Samaraweera and Jarlath Clifford for proofreading the text.

Before writing this book, we asked many children around the world to answer a questionnaire for us on nationality and statelessness. The wonderful answers of over two hundred children from various countries including Pakistan, the Netherlands, Serbia, Sri Lanka, the UK, the USA, Thailand and Ireland helped us immensely. We thank them all, as we do our partners and friends from around the world who collected these answers for us. Four children who answered the questionnaire are featured in the book: Lucas and Linde (the Netherlands) and Kithmi and Kenolee (Sri Lanka), but there were many other great answers as well!

This book is based on real people and their stories. It draws on research carried out by us and our partners, as well as research that has already been published. We are very grateful to everyone who shared their stories, as well as to everyone whose research helped us write this book:

❀ Kezia's character in Macedonia is based on research carried out by the Institute, the European Roma Rights Centre, the European Network on Statelessness and partner organisations on Roma statelessness in the Western Balkans, which was published in October 2017 *(see http://www.errc.org/cms/upload/file/roma-belong.pdf)*.

❀ Rosa's character in the Dominican Republic is based on the documentary film 'Our lives in Transit', published by Minority Rights Group International in April 2017 *(see https://www.youtube.com/watch?v=DAqGuj8AT1U)*.

❀ Grace and the other children in Cote d'Ivoire are based on a story published by UNHCR in November 2015 *(see http://kora.unhcr.org/lost-children-cote-divoire/)*.

❀ The story of Aasif, Riki and the Bajau Laut children draws on Helen Brunt's piece 'Stateless at Sea', published in the Institute's 2017 World's Stateless Report *(see http://www.institutesi.org/worldsstateless17.pdf)*.

❀ Sima's story in Germany is based on the report 'The Stateless Syrians' by Zahra Albarazi in 2013 *(see http://www.refworld.org/pdfid/52a983124.pdf)*, as well as interviews conducted in 2016 with stateless Syrian children, on file with the Institute.

❀ The story of the Makonde is based on the July 2017 documentary film 'The Journey of the Makonde to Citizenship' by the Kenya Human Rights Commission *(see https://www.youtube.com/watch?v=-PG8chfAX_U)*.

❀ The information from Nepal is based on the work of the Forum for Women Law and Development and our many interactions with Deepti Gurung and her family.

❀ The Questions by Stateless Children were first posed to the UN High Commissioner for Refugees and NGOs at the 2016 UNHCR-NGO Consultations in Geneva. (See Amal de Chickera, 'Being Accountable to Stateless Children and Youth' http://www.institutesi.org/worldsstateless17.pdf).

❀ The piece 'We See You' was written by Greg Constantine. A version of this was published in the Institute's 2017 World's Stateless Report (see http://www.institutesi.org/worldsstateless17.pdf).

❀ The 'Letter to a Stateless Child' was written by Linda Kerber, Rachel Brett and Stefanie Grant, all Trustees of the Institute.

Our gratitude also goes out to everyone who reviewed drafts of this book and provided invaluable advice, feedback and encouragement along the way. Tony Daly and Ciara Regan of 80:20 Educating and Acting for a Better World for being incredibly supportive throughout; Karl Ó Broin, Principal Maeve Tierney and other staff of St Cronan's BNS, Bray, Ireland; Samantha Pyper and her student Emily Antscherl of Al Yasmina Academy Abu Dhabi; Ms L. Browning, the Headteacher of Norbury Primary School Harrow, the UK; Ruwanthie de Chickera of Stages Theatre Group, Sri Lanka; Kerry Neal of UNICEF and Jo Holmwood and her colleagues at Kids Own Publishing.

We would also like to thank our donors whose support made this book possible: The Sigrid Rausing Trust, Janivo Stichting, Stichting Weeshius der Doopsgezinden and the Oak Foundation.

Finally, and most importantly, we would like to thank Neha, her sister Nikita, their mother Deepti and her partner Diwakar. Neha, for being the face of this book and the vehicle through which the story unfolds. The rest of her wonderful family for their continued dedication and commitment to fighting gender discriminatory nationality laws and statelessness in Nepal. You are an inspiration to us all.